By Nick Taylor

Although steam cars have not been made in quantity for over half a century, they are still remembered as very impressive machines. Driving one was simplicity itself, there being only a single lever on the steering column or a foot pedal to control speed and power. There were no clutch or gear shift to bother with, nor was there a complicated and expensive-to-repair automatic transmission either! In fact, most steamers did without a number of automotive parts, including spark plugs, carburetors, distributors, fly wheels, mufflers, tail pipes, drive shafts, universal joints, crank shafts, and timing gears. Later-model Stanleys claimed to have only 15 moving parts in the engine, 24 in the whole power plant, and only 37 moving parts in the entire car. There was a reverse pedal to depress for backing up, but in general, steamers seldom wore out parts and were as easy to drive as a modern car once one was under way.

At highway speeds the noise of wind rushing by was far louder than the faint puffing sound of the engine, and at a stop light there simply was not any sound at all. Steamers did not idle their engines to stop; they brought them to a complete halt, hence, no noise. Acceleration, likewise, was a quiet, smooth process limited only by the traction available at the rear wheels. It was even possible to step on the reverse pedal while traveling forward and spin the rear wheels backward, provided one took sufficient care not to be tossed through the windshield.

Before World War I it was common for manufacturers to enter their cars in racing and hill-climbing competitions. There were also endurance tests such as the famous Glidden Tours to impress the future car buyer who was more interested in reliability than power or speed. No mere publicity stunts, these events sent contestants through close to a thousand miles of impossible mountain roads. Steam cars were more than a match for their gasoline-engine competitors. In 1906 a Stanley could rightfully claim the title of "Fastest Car in the World" with its 127 miles per hour mark set at Ormond, Florida. White Sewing Machine Company's famous "Whistling Billy" steam racing car established a string of new track and hill-climbing

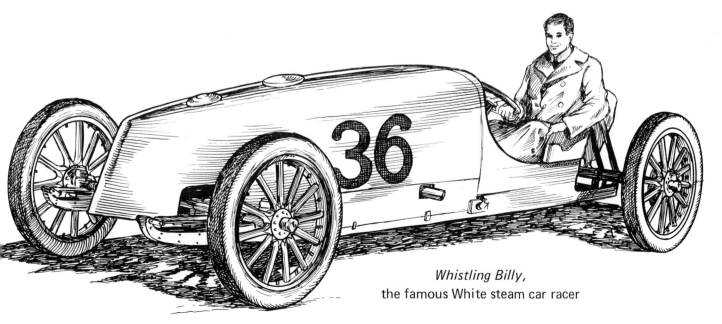

Whistling Billy,
the famous White steam car racer

records before 1910. The streamlined car, driven by Webb Jay, received its name from the unusual high-pitched exhaust sound it produced.

Powerful, silent, easy to drive, and proven in competition — all were true of the steam car, and yet they came and went in the short span of twenty years. Motoring around the turn of the century was a true adventure full of perils unknown to today's drivers. Roadways became virtual bogs offering hub cap-deep mud after a day's rain, and when dry, they turned into dust-filled ruts. Knowledgeable mechanics were a rarity, and as often as not, the local blacksmith had to suffice for repairs.

The first steam coach is credited to Julius Griffith, who offered the first regularly scheduled passenger service in 1822. Other coach services followed, including those of John Scott Russell, David Gordon, and Sir Goldworthy Gurney. In 1825 Gurney began regular service between Bath and London with a coach carrying six passengers inside and another twelve in open seats at 12½ miles per hour. Weighing 2 tons and using coke as fuel, it possessed a much more efficient engine design than earlier steam vehicles.

The work of Walter Handcock probably was the high point of the English steam carriage era. In all, Handcock built nine carriages bearing names such as "Automaton," "Era," and "Enterprise." Some were capable of 20 miles per hour, had double decks, and used a boiler pressure of 200 pounds. The Enterprise's boiler exploded due to a fireman's error on one occasion. In 1834 Handcock's coaches carried some 4,000 passengers in just under a 6-month period.

Walter Handcock's *Automaton,* 1834

Oddly enough, it was the promise and success of the steam coach that assured its end. Railroad and stage coach line owners mobilized to eliminate their dreaded competitors. Together they saw to it that public sentiment was turned against the steam coaches. From 1834 to 1839 steam buses came under public attack as a result of several accidents involving boiler explosions and loss of life. Parliament moved to limit the speed of steam carriages to 7 miles per hour. In addition, bridge and highway tolls were raised for the hapless buses. The final blow was struck in 1865 with the "Locomotives on Highways Act," or "Red Flag Law" as it is remembered, which required self-propelled vehicles to be preceded by a man on foot with a red warning flag by day and a red lantern at night. Steam car development in England came to a standstill until this law was repealed in 1896.

America was the home of several inventors who worked on steam cars in the mid- to late-19th century. Richard Dudgeon produced yet another of those "locomotives without wheels," contraptions that clanged and hissed over the streets of New York in the 1850's. Unlike the English steam carriages, however, Dudgeon's coach never achieved success. Perhaps the seating arrangement had something to do with this—the passengers sat on two bench-like seats directly on top of the hot horizontal boiler!

More important was the light-weight steam tricycle built in the 1880's by Lucius D. Copeland. Weighing but 220 pounds, the delicate-looking

Richard Dudgeon's steam carriage

Copeland's Steam Cycle, 1885

affair could travel at 10 miles per hour. Like its predecessors, Copeland's "Moto-Cycle" was doomed as a marketable product. The man of average means could not afford it, and the wealthy still preferred a handsome, traditional horse-drawn coach.

Even under the best conditions the gasoline-powered cars of the time were notoriously unreliable affairs. Hills that were climbed easily by a horse-drawn rig proved impossible for the underpowered horseless carriages. Cranking a stubborn gas engine was a back-breaking task. Once the car was under way, the driver needed great skill in managing the clutch, gear shift, and brakes so that the beast wouldn't stall. Smelly and noisy at best, these early cars were hardly motoring perfection, so it is not surprising that the steam car attracted an enthusiastic following. In fact, no less a person than Theodore Roosevelt used a White steamer during his administration. By 1906 White had sold over 1,400 cars.

What caused the demise of the steamer, or "peanut roaster" as they once were called? Folklore suggests that "vested interests kept them off the market," or that "one needed a locomotive engineer's license to operate [steamers]," or that "boilers were dangerous and likely to cause fires and explosions." All are untrue. No special license was ever required to drive a steamer, and boiler accidents were practically unknown, at least in the well-known makes. The steamer did have some drawbacks, but early motorists were willing to put up with them until the gas car was developed to a point which made the steamer too bothersome and expensive.

1909 White Model O touring car

What was it like to own a steam car? For one thing, steamers were always expensive. A 1907 White Model H Touring Car went for $2,500, and most of the Stanley models of 1913 were priced close to $2,000. Due to the economics of mass production, a comparable gas car sold for less. And in 1906 Henry Ford advertised his idea to sell cars for just $450.

The steamer owner's greatest cause of concern was likely to center around the care and feeding of the boiler, the device that turned water into steam. Most manufacturers placed the drum-shaped boiler under the hood, but White located it under the driver's seat, perhaps because it provided some degree of warmth there on chilly days. Boilers had few moving parts to wear out, but they were anything but simple. The Stanley design is a good example. A basic kerosene heater sent hot gases up a series of tubes (over 700 on some models) through the water space. The vast number of tubes was necessary in order to expose the water to as much heating surface as possible and help reduce the time to get up steam. Firing up a stone-cold Stanley involved heating up the pilot with an acetylene torch, lighting it, letting it warm up the main burner, turning on the kerosene, and once the main burner was lit, waiting for the boiler to build up steam pressure. Leaving the pilot burning continuously simplified the process considerably, but this always carried a certain risk, particularly if the car were stored in a fire trap of a livery stable.

The time to "steam up" a cold boiler could vary from 15 minutes to half an hour, depending on the skill of the operator. Once steam was up, various gadgets took care of letting in more water as steam was used by the engine, automatically shutting off the kerosene supply when pressure was adequate. On the road the main burner would turn on whenever steam pressure dropped. As long as the pilot was lit a car could be left standing for hours, requiring only letting off the hand brake and opening the throttle to leave the curb.

A variation of the Stanley-type boiler was used in the White steamer and originated with the French Serpollet. The "flash" boiler or water tube sent the water through the tubes and the hot gases about them. The amount of water to be heated up was very much reduced, and starting up a cold machine was much quicker. It did have the disadvantage, however, of not having a lot of steam in reserve for passing cars at high speed. Most boilers came swathed in insulating asbestos to cut down on heat loss. Stanley models were even wrapped in miles of high-strength piano wire, in much the same way as early cannons were reinforced.

With the early steamers the steam passed through the engine and was exhausted into the air. This meant water had to be replenished frequently. Stanleys had a nice feature to assist "watering up." A long rubber hose with a strainer at the end could be seen neatly coiled up near the right-side running board. The driver had only to place the end in a convenient horse trough or stream, and a pump run by the engine did the rest.

Poking around under a steamer is like looking through the plumbing section of a hardware store. Steam cars fairly bristled with valves and tubing. While these were not parts that wore out readily, they all served a necessary purpose and demanded periodic adjustment in order to keep a steam car healthy. For example, one didn't simply return from a trip, garage the steamer, and forget about it. First, the main burner had to be turned off, then the pilot valve, and finally, a steam valve was opened to let loose a cloud of white vapor — otherwise sediment and scales would collect in the boiler which would reduce mileage and possibly burn out the boiler.

Obviously, owning a steamer entailed a bit more than the sheer joy of driving one. When reliable electric self-starters made the gas car crank obsolete, when gas engines rumbled and roared less, and when a Model T Ford could be purchased for under $1,000, the steam car became simply too much of an inconvenience. Unfortunately, the greatest advantage of the steam car was not appreciated in its heyday. Steam cars used cheap grade fuel and did not pollute the air as much as internal-combustion gas and diesel engines. Neither feature was considered important in those days.

Could a man like Henry Ford have built a truly low-cost steam car? Will steam cars ever make a comeback? Steam car advocates are still plentiful, but these questions remain subjects of speculation.

1908 Stanley Model K
semi-racer takes on water

The history of the automobile began with a steam car of sorts. Nicolas Joseph Cugnot was a French army officer in 1763 when he began work on a machine to tow artillery pieces. The project was a government one sponsored by the Minister of War, the Marquis of Choiseul. A ponderous wooden tricycle set on a huge tea kettle-shaped boiler in the front was the result. Steam was fed by a copper pipe to two huge cylinders mounted over the single steerable front wheel.

Around 1769 or 1770, Cugnot's artillery tractor was demonstrated successfully before a gathering of high-ranking officers. We have no record of how well the tractor performed on this occasion, but history does note that later the vehicle was capable of 3 miles per hour and could haul 5 tons. The huge machine had an enormous appetite for steam, making it necessary to stop every fifteen minutes to allow the boiler to make more steam.

The rather dubious honor of being involved in the first automobile accident also belongs to Cugnot and his creation. The tractor struck and demolished a wall, overturning in the process. The Minister was disheartened by the accident, and as he was beset with financial problems caused by France's pre-revolutionary economic crises, he stopped all further experiments. Nothing more was heard from Cugnot, who died in 1804. It is known that at least two artillery tractors were built, the second being on display at the *Conservatoire des Arts et Métiers* in Paris.

The early history of the steam car and the steam locomotive was shaped by the work of a number of ingenious inventors who were all seeking a practical means of harnessing steam power for overland transportation. Among the first of these was Richard Trevithick (1771-1833), who is cred-

Nicolas Joseph Cugnot's
steam artillery tractor, 1770

ited with having built the first railroad locomotive to run on rails and the first steam threshing machine. In 1802 this enthusiastic English engineer built the first steam-powered carriage for carrying passengers. Weighing all of 8 tons, this machine could travel 10 miles per hour and was first demonstrated running about a small circular path where, for a modest fee, spectators could race the engine on foot. Later, Trevithick was to adapt the device for towing Londoners' carriages on brief trips. The denial of a much-needed Royal grant to continue his work meant that Trevithick's abilities were to remain unknown and unrewarded up to the time of his death.

America was not without its own steam pioneers, among them John Fitch, Nathaniel Read, and Oliver Evans. Evans' work is of particular interest. He built the first amphibious steam-powered dredge, *Orukter Amphibolus* in 1805 and actually drove it through the streets of Philadelphia and into the river. One can well imagine the curiosity of the crowd witnessing the travels of this 19-ton monster adorned with dredging gear and a paddle arrangement for water travel.

These ancestors of the steam car were really steam locomotives with the added burden of steering and without the benefit of a smooth railroad to distribute their enormous weight. In spite of these obstacles, the steam car seemed destined for a promising future in early 19th-century England. About the time Stephenson was operating the first railroad, McAdam was in the process of revolutionizing road building with a pavement which bears his name to this day. By the 1820's England was being crisscrossed with a marvelous network of flat, strong roads. This in turn led to a boom in the horse-drawn freight and passenger coach business. About the same time, a fleet of steam-driven coaches all sharing enormous size and weight, a boiler in the rear tended by one or more operators, the merest suggestion of brakes, and a driver up front to lend plenty of muscle to the crude steering wheel arrangement, took to the English roads. No fleeting experiments, these gaily decorated steam coaches were soon a cause of concern for the competing horse-drawn carriers and railroads.

The individually owned and operated steam car was not to come into its own until the close of the 1880's. It was not a matter of public acceptance nor of any one great invention that marked the event. Rather, a group of discoveries and inventions in other fields made it possible; tools, so to speak, which, in the hands of men like the Stanley brothers in America and Leon Serpollet in France, made the steam car a reality. Among the most important developments were the following: petroleum for use as a space- and weight-saving fuel and lubricant, tools to make close-fitting cylinders and pistons to provide efficient smaller engines of greater power, pneumatic tires to make travel over rough roads less of a bone-jarring ordeal, and steel of a predictable, uniform high strength so that things needn't be of huge proportions to be unbreakable. Ironically, these improvements also advanced the development of the gasoline engine, the steam car's ultimate enemy.

The Stanley brothers

By 1900 not quite twelve makes of steam cars had been marketed, and within a few years over twenty different brands were available. Grout, Lane, Meteor, and Toledo were a few of the many steam cars produced before 1920. None achieved the fame of the Stanley steamer nor were any produced in numbers rivaling the 18,000 Stanleys made up to 1925.

The Stanley steamer, the creation of twin brothers F. O. and F. E. Stanley and the first car to bear their name, was completed in 1897. The project was started the year before as a hobby; neither brother seriously considered going into the automobile business. At the time they were 48 years old and the owners of a prosperous company in Newton, Massachusetts which manufactured photographic dry plates. These were the forerunner of modern photographic film, and the Stanley Dry Plate was considered one of the best of its time. Possessing a rare combination of inventiveness, a shrewd business sense, and the skills to build just about anything, the brothers not only originated their own dry plate design but were the first to mass-produce violins as well. It is not surprising, then, to see how they were caught up in the enthusiasm for the new horseless carriages. By 1898 they had built two more cars, their only goal being to satisfy their curiosity about how much the design could be perfected.

That same year the first automobile show in nearby Boston was held. The Stanleys did not even bother to exhibit, but by then the sight of the identical twins silently steaming along the streets of Newton had created quite a stir, and at the invitation of the show's manager they agreed to enter a car in the outdoor speed trials and hill-climbing contest being held in conjunction with the show. The debut of the Stanley steamer was a smashing success. The car handily won both events, and its victory resulted in over a hundred orders for cars. Thus, regardless of their original intent, the brothers found themselves thrust into the steam car manufacturing business.

The Stanleys purchased an old bicycle factory next to their own plant. No sooner had they set up shop than they were approached by John Brisben

Walker, owner of *Cosmopolitan* magazine, with an offer to buy their infant automobile company. The Stanleys decided the best way of getting rid of pesky, would-be investors was simply to set an enormous price for their business. This they did, asking $250,000 in cash. To their amazement the terms were accepted, and on May 1, 1899 the brothers sold their business, agreeing not to manufacture steam cars for two years. As their own investment had been only $20,000, the Stanleys made quite a tidy profit.

The new company, which was named Locomobile, produced the Stanley design for two years. In the meantime, the brothers retreated to their workshop where they tinkered with a greatly improved steam car in preparation for the expiration of their agreed-upon two-year absence from the business. As it turned out, in May, 1901 Locomobile decided to abandon steam power in favor of the gas engine and sold the Stanleys back their factory, patents, and stock for $20,000. This, together with their advanced steam car design and a buying public eager for a reliable automobile, ensured their success for years to come.

Oddly enough, these two conservative Yankee businessmen shared a common enthusiasm for speed and were always ready to demonstrate the prowess of their cars. The publicity resulting from these exploits, of course,

1899 Locomobile

First Stanley racing car, 1903

was good for business, but the twins were never very concerned about generating sales. Nearly always behind on orders, they were content with the barest minimum of advertising and always felt that the craftsmanship they put into each of their cars was more important than the number they manufactured. The first Stanley racer must have seemed quite rakish in its day, with its low, streamlined look. Driven by F. E. Stanley, the car set a track record at Readville, Massachusetts on May 30, 1903, covering a mile in one minute and 2.8 seconds. That's just shy of 60 miles per hour and all with a 10 horsepower engine!

By 1905 the Stanleys had powered a car driven by Louis Ross that won the Dewar Cup, a world competition one-mile speed trial held on the beach at Ormond, Florida. The following year they entered a car of their own driven by Fred Marriot which set a world's record of 127.66 miles per hour. An amazing feat for 1906! Even more remarkable is the fact that the total weight of the car was only 1,600 pounds.

In 1907 the Stanleys returned to Ormond with an improved engine design and a boiler capable of much higher steam pressure. Unfortunately, winds had caused some waviness in the normally flat beach surface, but it was decided that conditions were still safe for attempting a new record. With Fred Marriot at the wheel, the sleek, low-slung car started from nine miles beyond the starting line and began to pick up speed. It must have been exciting to see this inverted boat-shaped car speeding along the ocean

1906 Stanley record-breaking racing car

with a minimum of noise. Marriot crossed the starting line at a speed no human had ever before attained. When the car reached the rough part of the course it left the ground suddenly, sailed a hundred feet in mid-air, turned slightly, and smashed into the hard-packed sand. The boiler, torn loose on impact, let out a resounding belch of steam and rolled a couple hundred feet down the beach. Marriot was unconscious but alive, though with several broken ribs, a bad cut on his head and one eye dangling from its socket. Miraculously, Marriot's eye was put back in, and eventually he regained perfect eyesight. It was estimated the car had been traveling 260 feet per second, over 175 miles per hour, at the time of the accident. The mishap gave the Stanleys second thoughts about future adventures of this sort. This was to be their last attempt at a speed record.

Before 1907 the Stanley steamer lost its "horseless carriage" look and sported the round-nosed, radiatorless hood bearing the brass Stanley name-plate which was to be its distinguishing mark until 1915. That year a condenser was added that looked exactly like the radiator of a conventional gas car. The new steamers also adopted balloon tires and followed the trend to closed, weathertight cars. From then on, Stanleys looked very much like gas cars.

In 1918 F. E. Stanley was steaming along the Newburyport Turnpike in Ipswich, Massachusetts and encountered two wagons blocking the road. He swerved off the road to avoid the wagons and was killed. F. O. Stanley

1908 Stanley Model J limousine

retired shortly thereafter, and the business went into decline. In 1925 the last Stanley steamer was built, and for all practical purposes, the era of the steam car was over.

The three biggest problems with all the earlier steam cars, including the Stanley, were that it took too much time and fussing over the boiler to get steam pressure up in a cold car, too many stops were needed to replenish the water supply, and boilers tended to form scale and deposits from minerals in the water which cut their efficiency and caused damage. While the Stanley brothers tended to compromise on these issues in order to keep the complexity and cost of their cars to a minimum, another gifted designer, Abner Doble, literally sought perfection in steam car design. He is remembered as the creator of the most elegant steam car of all — The Doble.

In 1903 Abner Doble was a boy of 8 working part-time as an apprentice in his father's San Francisco factory. The Stanley twins were 54 years old that year and were already launched in the steam car business. Like the Stanleys, Doble was a born mechanic and actually built his first steam car while a student at San Francisco's Lick High School, using a salvaged chassis, a fire tube boiler from a Locomobile, and an engine of his own design! The car was not a success, but it marked the beginning of a lifelong involvement with steam power for the young mechanic.

1909 Stanley Steamer Runabout

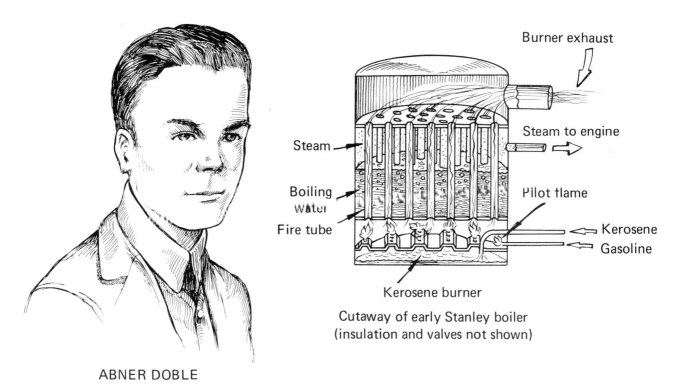

ABNER DOBLE

Burner exhaust

Steam

Boiling water

Fire tube

Steam to engine

Pilot flame

Kerosene

Gasoline

Kerosene burner

Cutaway of early Stanley boiler
(insulation and valves not shown)

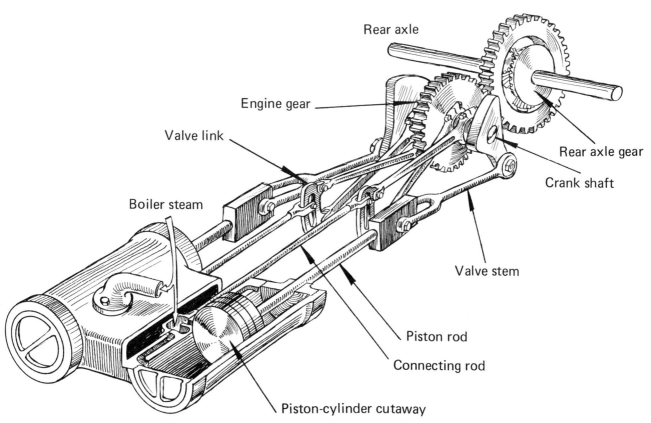

Rear axle

Engine gear

Valve link

Boiler steam

Rear axle gear

Crank shaft

Valve stem

Piston rod

Connecting rod

Piston-cylinder cutaway

Stanley engine with only moving parts shown

Doble attended Massachusetts Institute of Technology in later years, but it was apparent that he did not favor the academic approach to design. In his first year Doble spent all his spare time working on steam car design at a machine shop in Waltham, Massachusetts. He met the Stanley brothers in nearby Newton and disagreed with them on the practicality of a quick-starting, easy-to-operate boiler and on the possibility of reducing water consumption. Doble was convinced both problems could be solved, so he set about to find their solutions. He built five cars in all, improving as he went along, and named the fifth "Doble Model A" in 1912. He showed the car to the Stanleys who were so impressed with the condenser (the water-conserving device) that they began to work on a version of the same device for their own products.

On the success of the Model A, Doble left M.I.T. after two years and built his Model B in 1914. With its improved condenser the range between water stops for the steamer was extended to 300 miles. A few years earlier it was not unusual for a steamer to have to refill the water tank every 50 to 75 miles. The other important new feature was a much-improved boiler burner that reduced the time and effort involved in getting up steam pressure.

Setting off on a tour of industrial cities in his Model B, Doble sought an engineering job with a company willing to produce his car. In 1915 he ended up in Detroit working for the Chalmers Motor Company (later to become a part of Chrysler). The next year General Engineering Company offered to build his design in limited numbers. The car, which was called the Doble Detroit, seemed to be the ultimate in steam cars.

The Doble Detroit had a sparkplug-ignited, blower-type burner that was far superior to the Stanley pilot flame burner. The basic design much

Doble Model A, Abner Doble's first condensing steam car, built in his sparetime while at M.I.T.

resembles that in common use in oil-fired home heating furnaces today. Later, in fact, it was adapted for this use and sold under the label "No Kol House Heating Burner." An ad which boasted a two-minute start-up time with the mere turning of a switch further stated that if the car had been run at all within the past two hours there would be sufficient warmth in the engine to guarantee an immediate start. True, the price was a hefty $3,750 - about twice the price of the average gas car — but even so, prospects looked good for the new car. Unfortunately, only three Doble Detroits were ever built. With the outbreak of World War I the government's War Emergency Board stopped production to conserve steel for vital war-related industries. This was the first of several setbacks affecting Abner Doble's career.

It is interesting to speculate what the Doble Detroit's future might have been had this unfortunate turn of events not taken place. The car was shown at the 1917 New York Automobile Show held just before America's entry into the war. Public response was sensational. A few days after the show, the Postal Service refused to deliver the mountains of letters that were coming in and asked that they be picked up instead. Over 50,000 letters and 700 telegrams came in from dealers wanting to sell the car, prospective buyers, and persons who wanted to buy stock in the company. Actual orders for over 10,000 cars were received in ninety days.

Doble spent the war years working on a better steam car design, and in 1920 he and his three brothers organized the Doble Steam Motors Company. By 1922 they were working on the latest Model D in a small shop on Harrison Street in San Francisco. The goal set for the Model D Doble seems overly ambitious even by present-day standards. Each car was guaranteed for 100,000 miles and billed as requiring no water before 2,000 to 3,000 miles! Furthermore, the start-up time of a cold car was guaranteed not to exceed 30 seconds.

Only five cars were built in San Francisco by 1923, but they were impressive enough to attract investors. A grand new factory and first-class manufacturing operation was planned for Emeryville, California. It seemed that Abner Doble's ship was about to come in at last.

The new factory opened in January, 1924 with a capacity to turn out 300 cars per year with room to expand that to 1,000 cars per year. Doble had to make only 50 cars, and under the terms of the financing arrangement it would be possible to sell more stock and bring in much-needed money.

The Emeryville Dobles were called Model E's, and as with prior models, they reflected their builder's dedication to producing the finest steam car imaginable. As a result, they were neither lightweight nor cheap. The cars weighed from 3,900 to 4,550 pounds. Doble manufactured only the chassis, which sold for $6,000, and had custom bodies fitted by the respected builder, Murphy of Pasadena, California, for an additional $2,850 to $3,750. For a car of this class the Model E was not unduly expensive, especially given the level of its performance and the workmanship that went into it.

Indeed, many felt the car, which handled the steepest hill with ease and could reach 85 miles per hour, was a true bargain.

Two discouraging events limited production of the Model E to a mere 37 cars from 1924 to 1932. No sooner had the operation begun than it was discovered that an inexperienced driver, under certain circumstances, could cause serious damage to the boiler. Given the 100,000-mile guarantee, the prospect of having to replace countless damaged boilers spelled financial disaster for the company. Production was stopped and Abner Doble set about finding a solution to the problem.

What next unfolded was a financial and legal horror story which ultimately finished the Doble. Inquiries from stockholders were being made regarding when stocks would be received and dividends forthcoming. To Doble's dismay no record of these individuals as stockholders could be found. It turned out that the company's agents had been selling shares illegally and pocketing the cash. A tangle of law suits followed which essentially reduced the firm to bankruptcy. Still, Abner Doble persevered and managed to redesign the boiler so that any danger from improper use by inexperienced drivers was eliminated. Doble paid off his debts to the frustrated stockholders from his own pocket, but by 1928 the firm was broke, even though it had one of the best steam car designs ever created and all the valuable patents to protect itself from competition.

Under the hood of a Doble Model E

1925 Doble Series E coupe

One last calamity was to befall the Doble: the great stock market crash of 1929. This unfortunate event dealt the final blow to Abner Doble's appeals for new investment dollars. Some money was obtained from licenses sold to other firms for the use of Doble patents, and a few Model F's were produced, but these supplied only the power source; the chassis were made by other car builders. The Doble company folded in 1932.

Abner Doble was active as a consultant on projects using mobile steam power until his death in 1961. Buses and trucks were produced using the Doble designs in New Zealand, England, and Germany during the 1930's. None could ever quite compete in cost with the mass-produced diesel engine which was coming into its own at the time.

1925 Doble Phaeton

Steam Car Model

Tools Required: Sharp scissors, fast drying cement, a ruler & a dull knife.
Color parts before cutting out. Use felt tip pens, colored pencils or crayons.

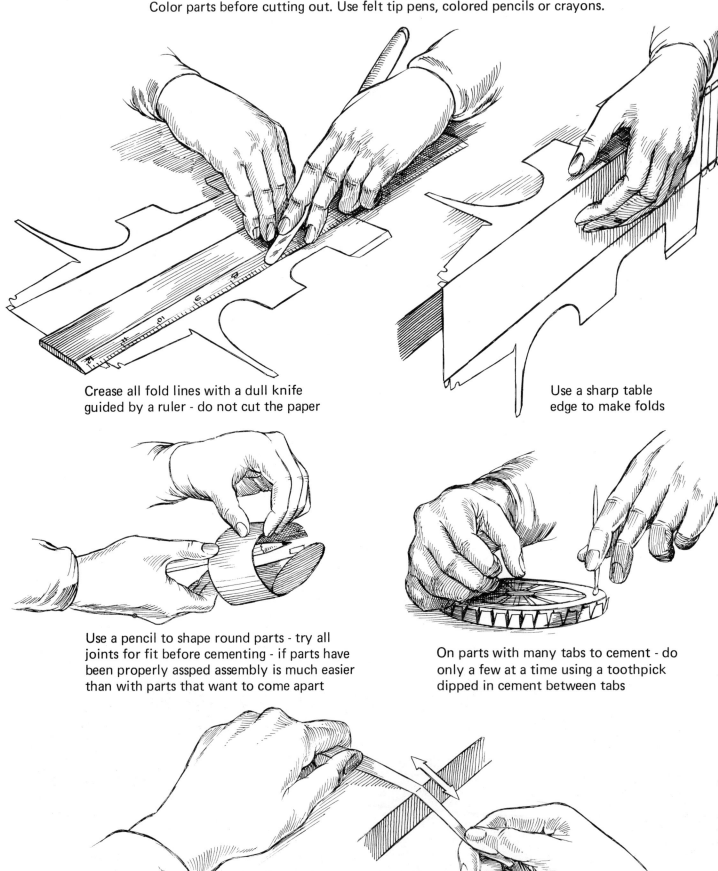

Crease all fold lines with a dull knife
guided by a ruler - do not cut the paper

Use a sharp table
edge to make folds

Use a pencil to shape round parts - try all
joints for fit before cementing - if parts have
been properly assped assembly is much easier
than with parts that want to come apart

On parts with many tabs to cement - do
only a few at a time using a toothpick
dipped in cement between tabs

Before wrapping parts around toothpicks, first curl the paper by rubbing
it over a sharp table edge as shown.

1909 *Stanley Runabout*
Instructions

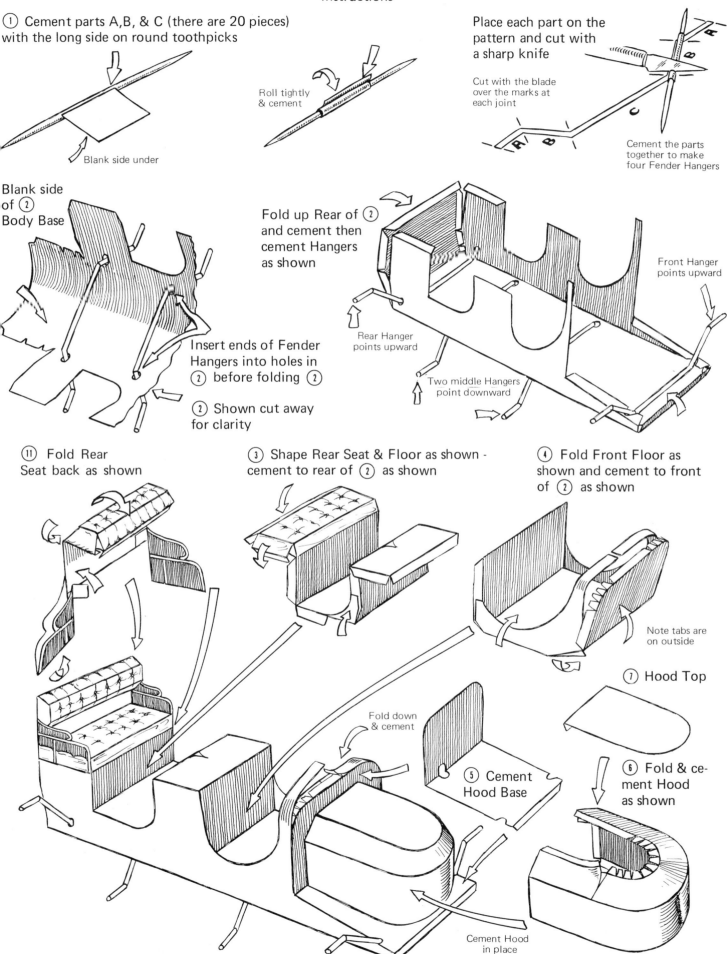

① Cement parts A, B, & C (there are 20 pieces) with the long side on round toothpicks

Blank side under

Roll tightly & cement

Place each part on the pattern and cut with a sharp knife

Cut with the blade over the marks at each joint

Cement the parts together to make four Fender Hangers

Blank side of ② Body Base

Fold up Rear of ② and cement then cement Hangers as shown

Front Hanger points upward

Rear Hanger points upward

Two middle Hangers point downward

Insert ends of Fender Hangers into holes in ② before folding ②

② Shown cut away for clarity

⑪ Fold Rear Seat back as shown

③ Shape Rear Seat & Floor as shown - cement to rear of ② as shown

④ Fold Front Floor as shown and cement to front of ② as shown

Note tabs are on outside

⑦ Hood Top

Fold down & cement

⑤ Cement Hood Base

⑥ Fold & cement Hood as shown

Cement Hood in place

1909 *Stanley Runabout*
Instructions

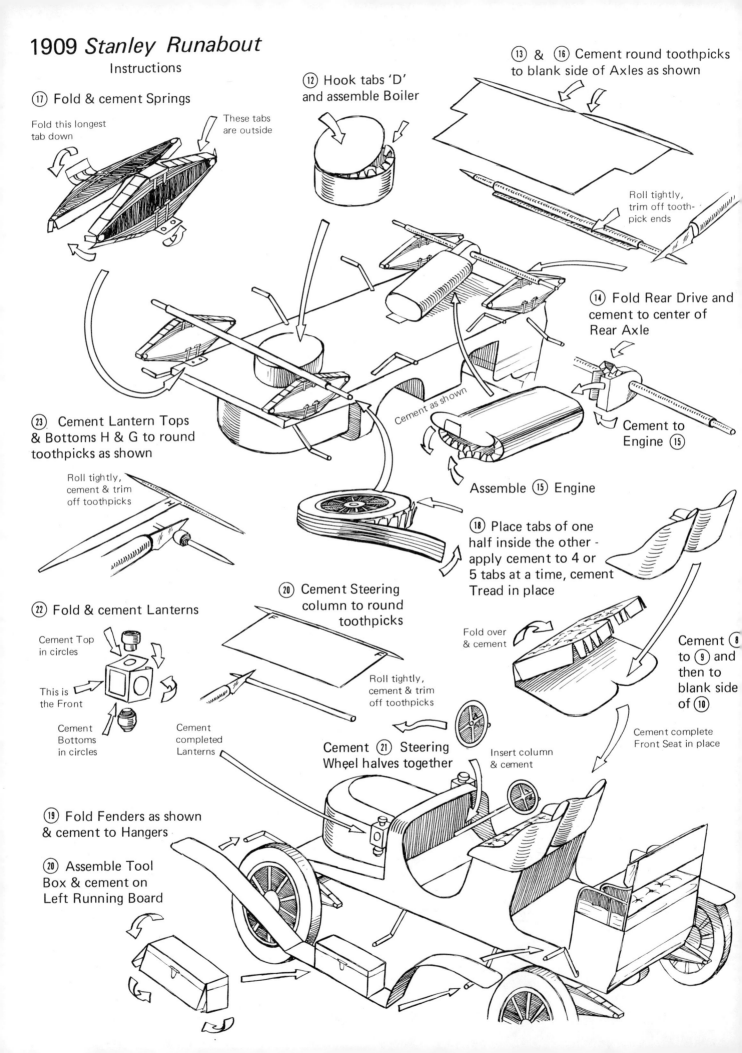

⑰ Fold & cement Springs

Fold this longest tab down

These tabs are outside

⑫ Hook tabs 'D' and assemble Boiler

⑬ & ⑯ Cement round toothpicks to blank side of Axles as shown

Roll tightly, trim off toothpick ends

⑭ Fold Rear Drive and cement to center of Rear Axle

Cement to Engine ⑮

⑬ Cement Lantern Tops & Bottoms H & G to round toothpicks as shown

Roll tightly, cement & trim off toothpicks

Cement as shown

Assemble ⑮ Engine

⑱ Place tabs of one half inside the other - apply cement to 4 or 5 tabs at a time, cement Tread in place

Fold over & cement

Cement ⑧ to ⑨ and then to blank side of ⑩

Cement complete Front Seat in place

⑫ Fold & cement Lanterns

Cement Top in circles

This is the Front

Cement Bottoms in circles

Cement completed Lanterns

⑳ Cement Steering column to round toothpicks

Roll tightly, cement & trim off toothpicks

Cement ㉑ Steering Wheel halves together

Insert column & cement

⑲ Fold Fenders as shown & cement to Hangers

⑳ Assemble Tool Box & cement on Left Running Board

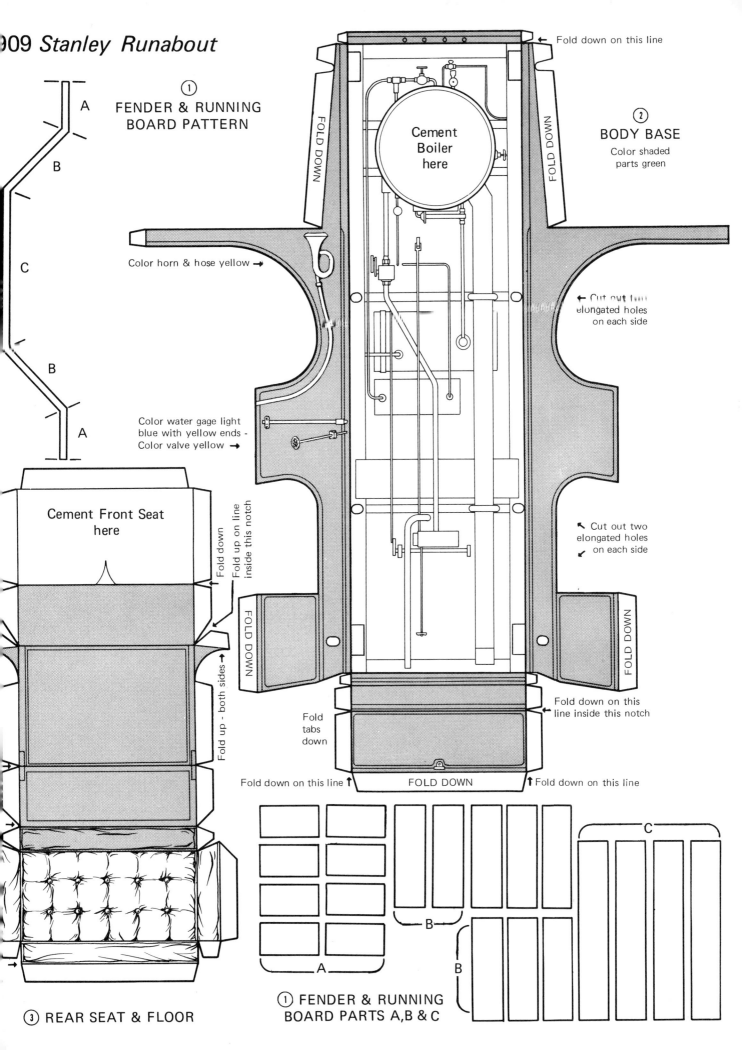

1909 *Stanley Runabout*

① FENDER & RUNNING BOARD PATTERN

A

B

C

B

A

← Fold down on this line

FOLD DOWN

FOLD DOWN

Cement Boiler here

② BODY BASE

Color shaded parts green

Color horn & hose yellow →

← Cut out two elongated holes on each side

Color water gage light blue with yellow ends - Color valve yellow →

↖ Cut out two elongated holes ↙ on each side

Cement Front Seat here

Fold down

Fold up on line inside this notch

Fold up - both sides ↑

FOLD DOWN

FOLD DOWN

Fold tabs down

Fold down on this line inside this notch

Fold down on this line ↑   FOLD DOWN   ↑ Fold down on this line

③ REAR SEAT & FLOOR

C

B

A

B

① FENDER & RUNNING BOARD PARTS A, B & C

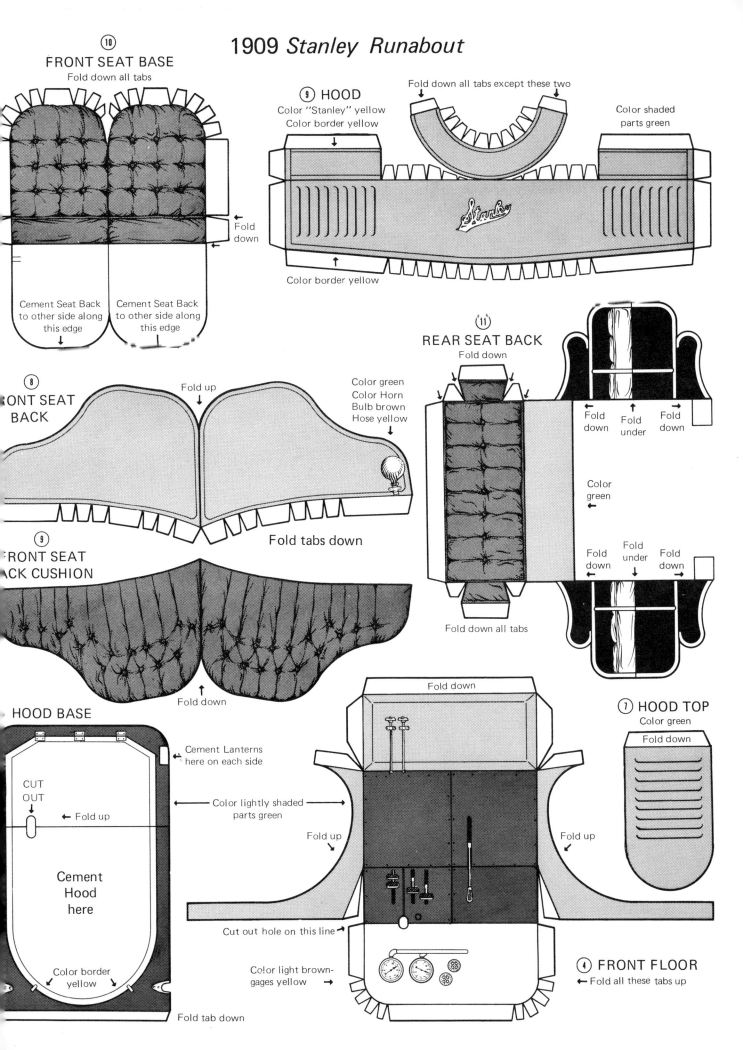

1909 *Stanley Runabout*

⑩ **FRONT SEAT BASE**
Fold down all tabs

Cement Seat Back to other side along this edge

Cement Seat Back to other side along this edge

⑨ **HOOD**
Color "Stanley" yellow
Color border yellow

Fold down all tabs except these two

Color shaded parts green

Stanley

Color border yellow

← Fold down

⑧ **FRONT SEAT BACK**

Fold up

Color green
Color Horn Bulb brown
Hose yellow

Fold tabs down

⑪ **REAR SEAT BACK**
Fold down

Fold down Fold under Fold down

Color green ←

Fold down Fold under Fold down

Fold down all tabs

⑨ **FRONT SEAT BACK CUSHION**

Fold down

HOOD BASE

CUT OUT

← Fold up

Cement Hood here

Cement Lanterns here on each side

Color lightly shaded parts green

Fold up

Color border yellow

Fold tab down

Fold down

Fold up

Cut out hole on this line ►

Color light brown-gages yellow →

⑦ **HOOD TOP**
Color green

Fold down

Fold up

④ **FRONT FLOOR**
← Fold all these tabs up

909 *Stanley Runabout*

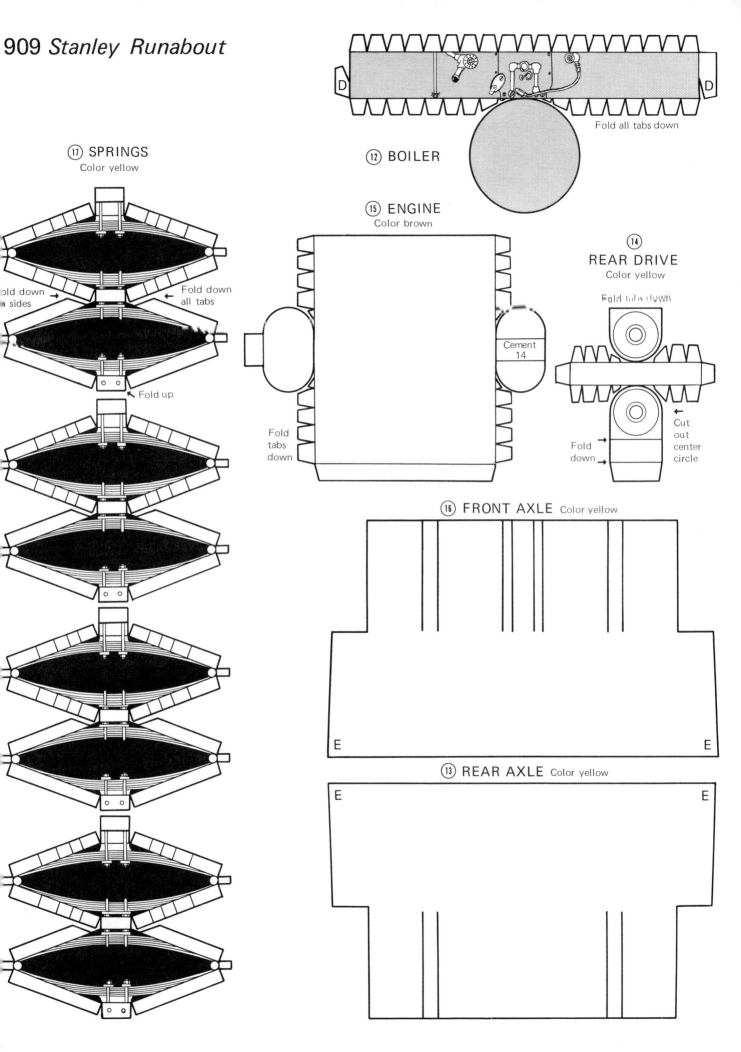

12 BOILER

Fold all tabs down

17 SPRINGS
Color yellow

Fold down sides

Fold down all tabs

Fold up

15 ENGINE
Color brown

Cement 14

Fold tabs down

14 REAR DRIVE
Color yellow

Fold tabs down

Fold down

Cut out center circle

D   D

16 FRONT AXLE Color yellow

E   E

13 REAR AXLE Color yellow

E   E

1909 *Stanley Runabout*

TIRE TREAD

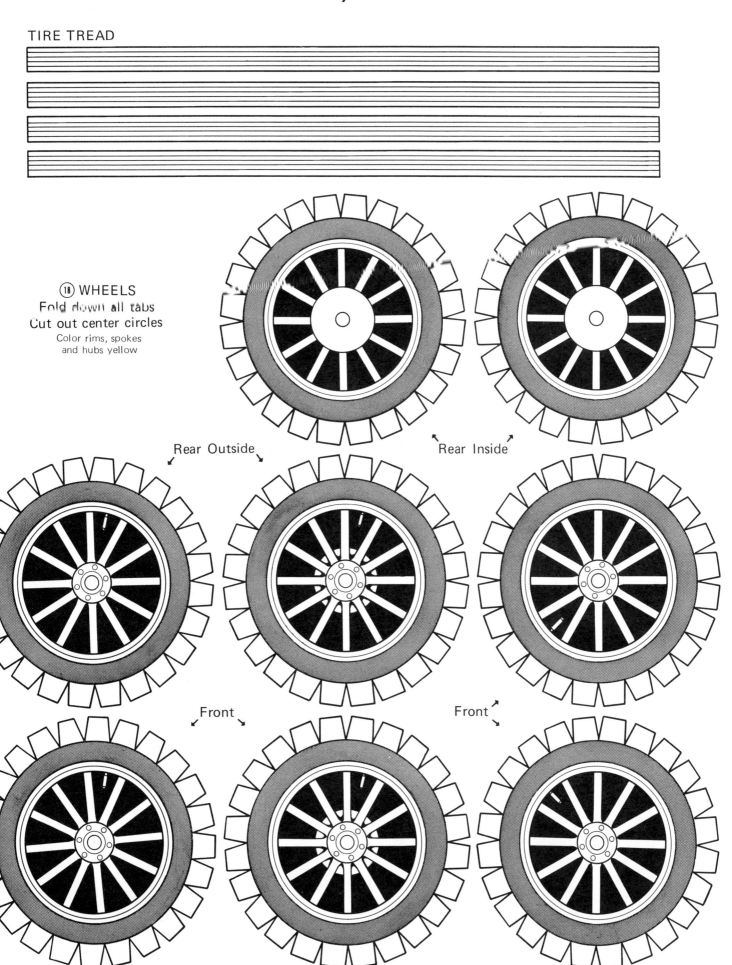

⑱ **WHEELS**
Fold down all tabs
Cut out center circles
Color rims, spokes
and hubs yellow

Rear Outside

Rear Inside

Front

Front

1909 *Stanley Runabout*

(20) **STEERING COLUMN**

F

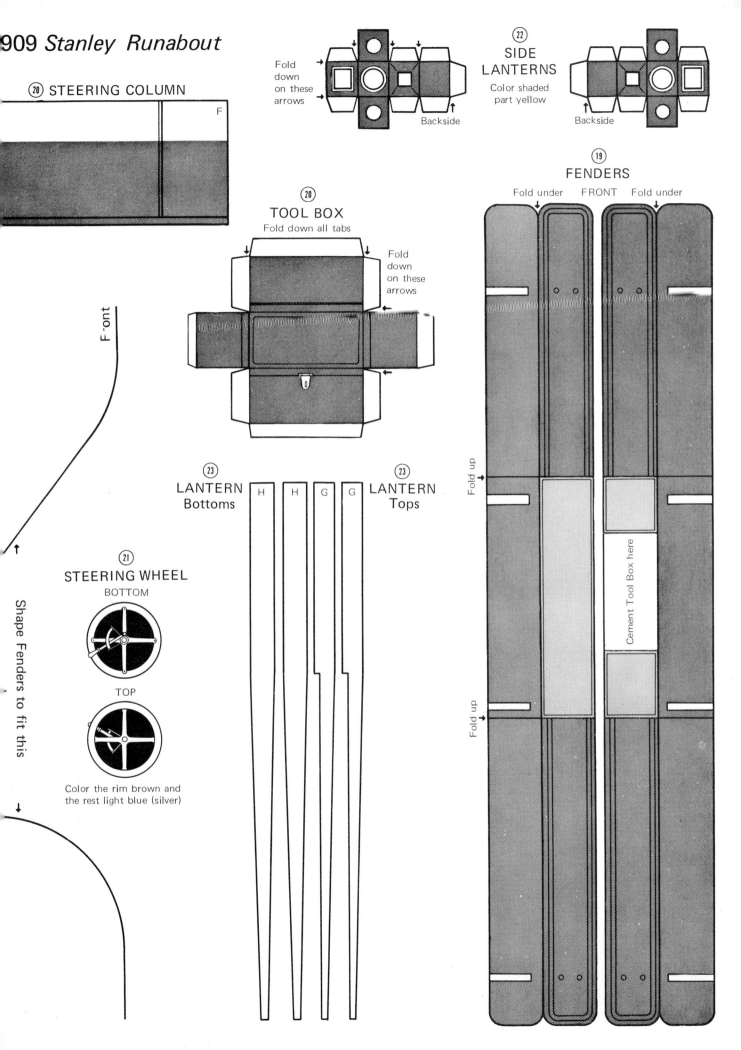

Fold down on these arrows

Backside

(22) **SIDE LANTERNS**

Color shaded part yellow

Backside

(19) **FENDERS**

Fold under   FRONT   Fold under

Fold up ➝

Fold up ➝

Cement Tool Box here

(20) **TOOL BOX**

Fold down all tabs

Fold down on these arrows

Front

Shape Fenders to fit this

(23) **LANTERN Bottoms**

H   H   G   G

(23) **LANTERN Tops**

(21) **STEERING WHEEL**

BOTTOM

TOP

Color the rim brown and the rest light blue (silver)

399 *Locomobile*
Instructions

Fold body & cement as shown

② Fold inside body as shown, place a small dot of cement on four corners then use a toothpick to cement tabs in place

Roll & cement Boiler Stack - cement rectangular base & cement to place on body marked 'A'

① Cement seat back in place

④ Fold Seat back, double then cement to the inside of ③

sert rolled strips cement in place

Lanterns cemented to square on body

Roll round Lantern parts as shown, cement tabs

Roll tightly, cement & trim off ends of toothpick

⑥ Shape Seat Bottom, then cement tabs place on body as shown

⑨ Make two Axles - cement toothpicks to blak side edge shown - roll tightly, cement & trim toothpick off

⑧ Cement round toothpicks to blank side edge of Lantern strips as shown

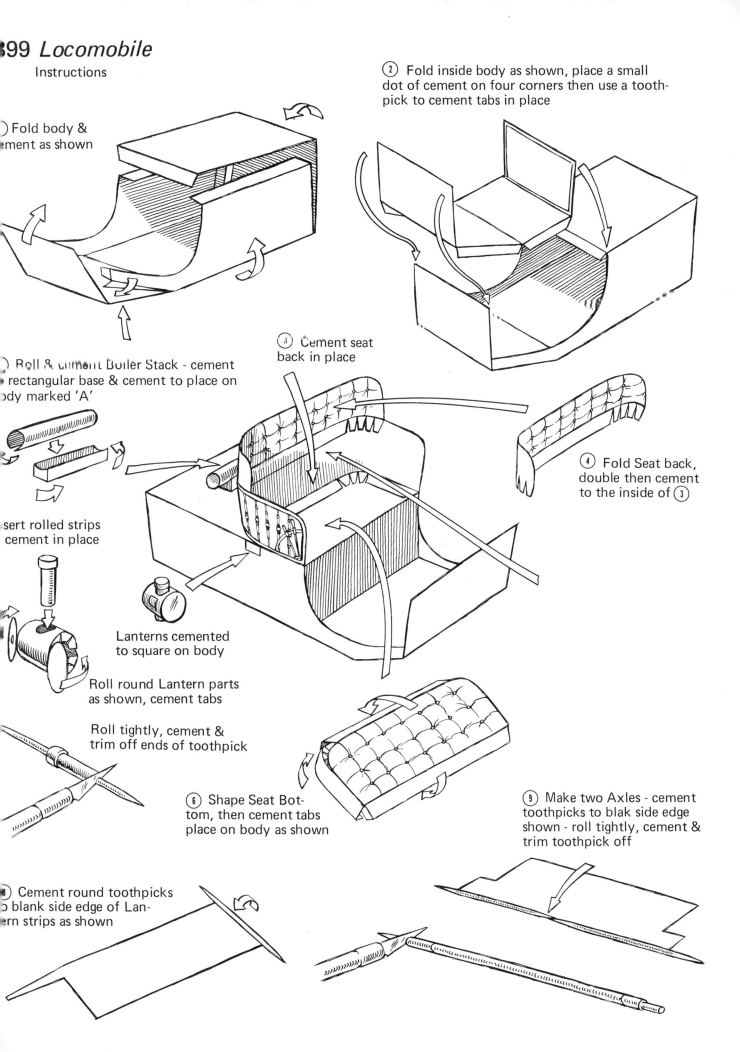

1899 *Locomobile*

Instructions

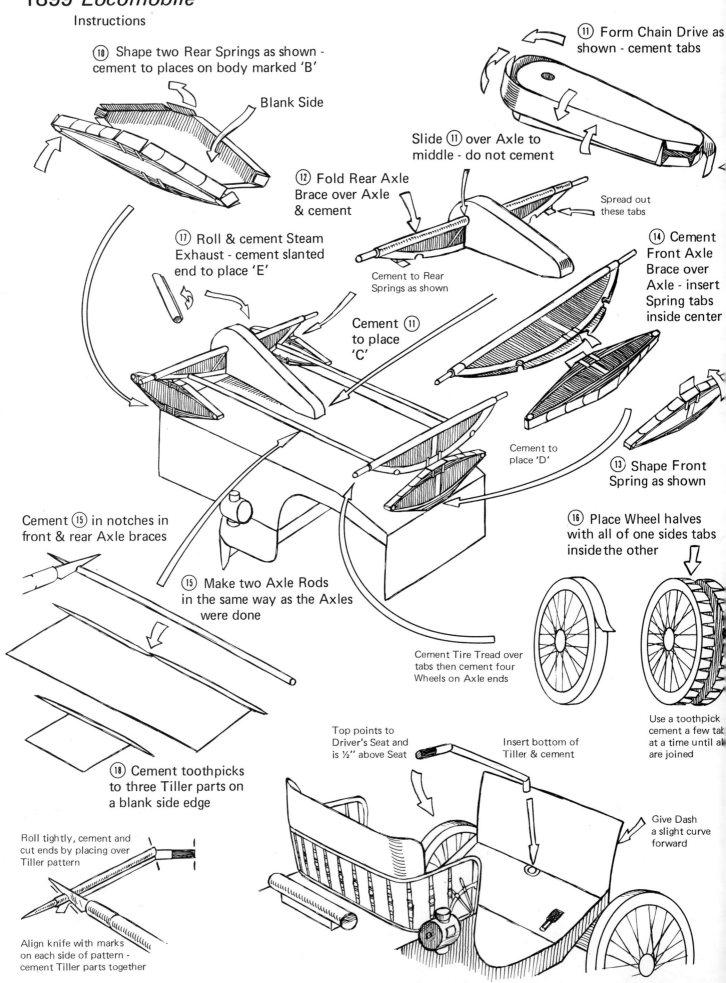

⑩ Shape two Rear Springs as shown - cement to places on body marked 'B'

Blank Side

⑪ Form Chain Drive as shown - cement tabs

Slide ⑪ over Axle to middle - do not cement

⑫ Fold Rear Axle Brace over Axle & cement

Spread out these tabs

⑭ Cement Front Axle Brace over Axle - insert Spring tabs inside center

Cement to Rear Springs as shown

⑰ Roll & cement Steam Exhaust - cement slanted end to place 'E'

Cement ⑪ to place 'C'

Cement to place 'D'

⑬ Shape Front Spring as shown

Cement ⑮ in notches in front & rear Axle braces

⑯ Place Wheel halves with all of one sides tabs inside the other

⑮ Make two Axle Rods in the same way as the Axles were done

Cement Tire Tread over tabs then cement four Wheels on Axle ends

Use a toothpick cement a few tab at a time until al are joined

⑱ Cement toothpicks to three Tiller parts on a blank side edge

Top points to Driver's Seat and is ½" above Seat

Insert bottom of Tiller & cement

Give Dash a slight curve forward

Roll tightly, cement and cut ends by placing over Tiller pattern

Align knife with marks on each side of pattern - cement Tiller parts together

1899 *Locomobile*

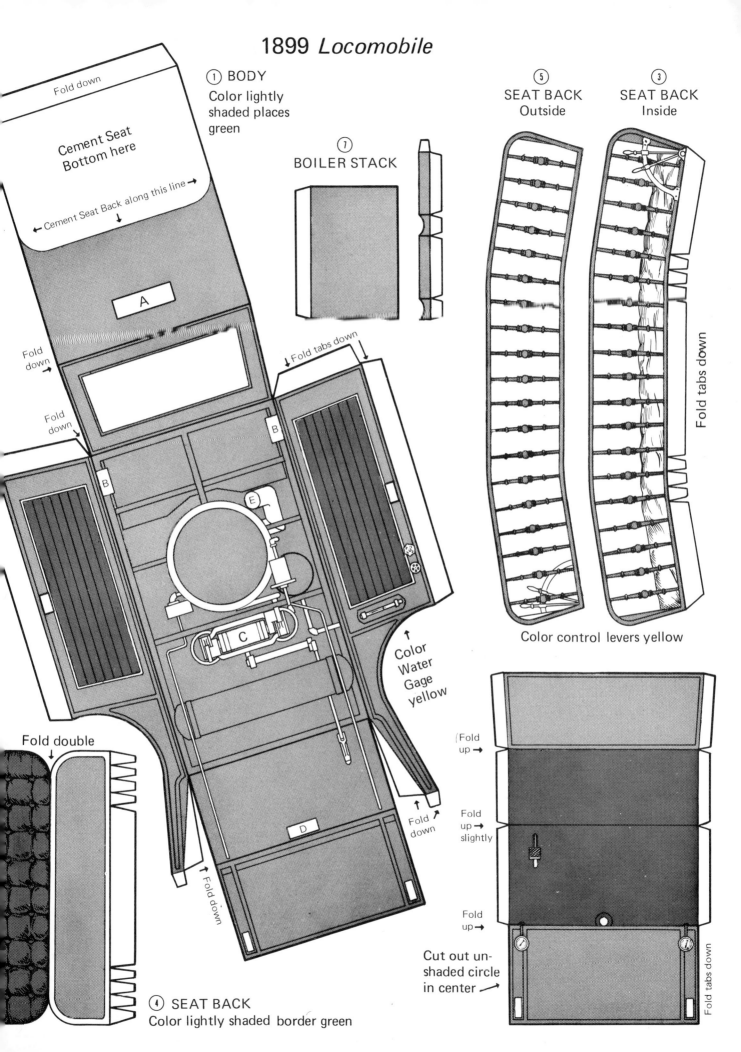

① BODY
Color lightly
shaded places
green

Fold down

Cement Seat
Bottom here

← Cement Seat Back along this line →

A

Fold
down →

Fold
down →

B

B

E

C

D

⑦
BOILER STACK

↓ Fold tabs down

↓ Fold tabs down

Fold
down

↑
Color
Water
Gage
yellow

↓
Fold
down ↗

Fold double

④ SEAT BACK
Color lightly shaded border green

⑤
SEAT BACK
Outside

③
SEAT BACK
Inside

Fold tabs down

Color control levers yellow

(Fold
up →

Fold
up →
slightly

Fold
up →

Cut out un-
shaded circle
in center →

Fold tabs down

1899 *Locomobile*

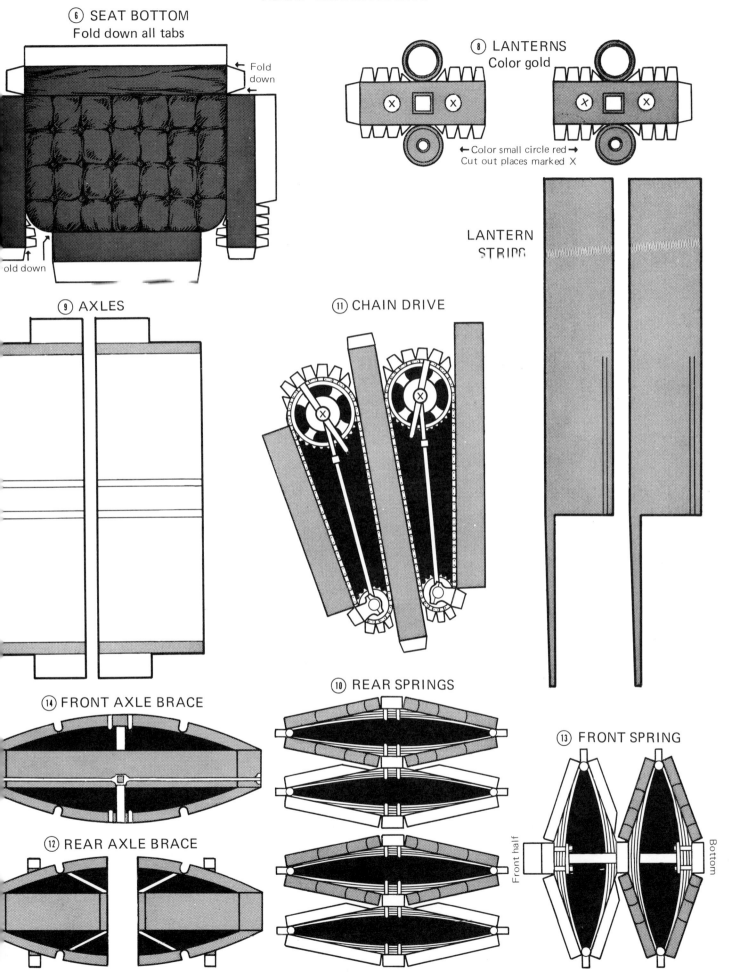

⑥ SEAT BOTTOM
Fold down all tabs

Fold down

old down

⑧ LANTERNS
Color gold

← Color small circle red →
Cut out places marked X

LANTERN STRIPS

⑨ AXLES

⑪ CHAIN DRIVE

⑭ FRONT AXLE BRACE

⑩ REAR SPRINGS

⑬ FRONT SPRING

Front half

Bottom

⑫ REAR AXLE BRACE